Tomás's Birthday Treasure!

Adapted by Frank Berrios • Illustrated by Sarah Jaques
Based on the episode "Tomás's Birthday Surprise" written by JP Meier

 **A GOLDEN BOOK • NEW YORK**

© 2022 Viacom International Inc. All Rights Reserved. Nickelodeon, Santiago of the Seas, and all related titles, logos, and characters are trademarks of Viacom International Inc. Published in the United States by Golden Books, an imprint of Random House Children's Books, a division of Penguin Random House LLC, 1745 Broadway, New York, NY 10019, and in Canada by Penguin Random House Canada Limited, Toronto. Golden Books, A Golden Book, A Little Golden Book, the G colophon, and the distinctive gold spine are registered trademarks of Penguin Random House LLC.

rhcbooks.com

ISBN 978-0-593-12765-0 (trade)

T#: 867064

Printed in the United States of America

10 9 8 7 6 5 4 3 2 1

Santiago, Abuelo, and Lorelai were up early one morning. They had lots to do—it was Tomás's birthday!

"¡Hola, Captain Sprinkles!" said Santiago as he hopped off his ship, *El Bravo.*

"Ahoy, mateys! Yer just in time!" replied the captain, revealing his latest masterpiece—a beautiful cake shaped like a treasure chest!

"That's the coolest cake I've ever seen!" said Santiago. "It looks like real gold!"

"Aye, it be me special *tres leches* cake," Captain Sprinkles replied proudly. "Covered in me rare gold frosting!"

"*Tres leches* is Tomás's favorite cake!"
said Santiago.

"And gold is his favorite treasure!" added
Lorelai. It was going to be the perfect
birthday surprise for Tomás.

Santiago, Lorelai, and Abuelo headed back to *El Bravo.*

"If yer looking for a shortcut, sail left of them rocks. Just don't go into the fog," Captain Sprinkles called after them. "That be . . . El Mar Malo!"

Lorelai gasped. "The Bad Sea?" she asked.

"Legend says it's full of magical dangers!" said Abuelo. "Even El Pulpo Gigante!"

"The Giant Octopus?" asked Santiago.

"Aye!" said Captain Sprinkles. "So steer clear of the fog. No creature on the High Seas can resist a Captain Sprinkles cake!"

As they set sail, no one noticed that Bonnie Bones was watching them.

"A solid gold treasure chest!" she said, looking at the cake. "Soon enough, that treasure will be mine!"

Meanwhile, back on Isla Encanto, Tomás was looking for his birthday party.

"Where is everyone?" he asked his sister, Tina.

"You'll have to get all the pieces of the map to find them!" she replied.

"A treasure hunt to find my birthday party?" asked Tomás. "I love it!"

They raced off to find the next piece of the map.

Back on *El Bravo*, Santiago
and the crew felt something
bump the ship. It was Bonnie Bones
in her ship, *El Calamar*!

"Finders keepers!" she said as she swooped
in and snatched the birthday cake.

"Prickly prawns!" said Lorelai. "Bonnie took the cake!"

"And she's taking it right into El Mar Malo!" added Abuelo.

"Shiver me timbers! We'd better get in there before it's too late!" said Santiago. "Good pirates always do what's right!"

They sailed after Bonnie Bones and Tomás's birthday cake.

"Avast, Bonnie! This is El Mar Malo. You have to leave!" Santiago warned her.

"And give us back Tomás's cake!" called Abuelo.

"Cake? You can't trick me! I know treasure when I see it!" replied Bonnie.

Suddenly, her ship sailed into a sea of bubbles.
The bubbles were so big that both ships began
to bounce! Santiago used the power of
El Bravo to jump safely over
the bubbles.

"Bonnie Bones, stop! That's not treasure—
it's a cake!" said Santiago.

"Nice try!" replied Bonnie. "Nobody's taking
this treasure from me."

Suddenly, huge tentacles reached out of
the ocean and grabbed her. It was the
Giant Octopus!

El Pulpo Gigante took the cake!
"It *is* just a cake!" Bonnie said. "No cake is
worth this much trouble!" She quickly escaped.

The brave Pirate Protector Santiago would not give up easily. He swung through the air and snatched the cake from the Giant Octopus. But before he could get back to his ship, the octopus snagged *him*!

"*¡Por favor!* Please!" said Santiago. "It's my cousin's birthday cake!"

Suddenly, Santiago had an idea! He sliced
off a piece of the cake and gave it to the
Giant Octopus.

"Try this," he said.

El Pulpo Gigante took the slice and quickly
gobbled it up. The sea creature thought it
was yummy!

The Giant Octopus placed Santiago and the rest of the cake back on *El Bravo*. Lorelai and Abuelo were shocked!
"How did you know he only wanted some cake?" asked Abuelo.
"No creature on the High Seas can resist a Captain Sprinkles cake, remember?" laughed Santiago.

At the pier, Tomás had found the last map piece. When he put the map together, he saw it was shaped like *El Bravo*!

"My party is on *El Bravo*?" he asked.

"*¡Sí!*" replied Tina as the boat sailed into view.

"Surprise! Happy birthday, Tomás!" cheered Santiago and the crew while he and Tina climbed aboard.

"A golden cake just for you, *primo*," said Santiago.

"Whoa! *¿¡Tres leches!?* My favorite!" replied Tomás. "No creature on the High Seas can resist a Captain Sprinkles cake!"

"You have no idea," chuckled Santiago.

Everyone enjoyed the delicious birthday party treat!